Blind Children by Israel Zangwill

Israel Zangwill was born in London on 21st January 1864, to a family of Jewish immigrants from the Russian Empire.

Zangwill was initially educated in Plymouth and Bristol. At age 9 he was enrolled in the Jews' Free School in Spitalfields in east London. Zangwill excelled here. He began to teach part-time at the school and eventually full time. Whilst teaching he also studied with the University of London and by 1884 had earned his BA with triple honours in philosophy, history, and the sciences.

His writing earned him the sobriquet "the Dickens of the Ghetto" primarily based on his much lauded novel 'Children of the Ghetto: A Study of a Peculiar People' in 1892 and its glimpse of the poverty-stricken life in London's Jewish quarter.

As a writer he was keen to reflect on his political and social outlooks. His simulation of Yiddish sentence structure in English aroused great interest. His mystery work, 'The Big Bow Mystery' (1892) was the first locked room mystery novel.

Zangwill was also involved with narrowly focused Jewish issues as an assimilationist, an early Zionist, and later a territorialist. In the early 1890s he had joined the Lovers of Zion movement in England. In 1897 he joined Theodor Herzl (considered the father of modern political Zionism) in founding the World Zionist Organization.

Zangwill quit the established philosophy of Zionism when his plan for a homeland in Uganda was rejected and founded his own organisation; the Jewish Territorialist Organization. Its stated goal was to create a Jewish homeland in whatever territory in the world could be found for them.

Amongst the challenges in his life he found time to write poetry. He had translated a medieval Jewish poet in 1903 and his volume 'Blind Children' in 1908 shows his promise in this new endeavour.

'The Melting Pot' in 1909 made Zangwill's name as an admired playwright. When the play opened in Washington D.C., former President Theodore Roosevelt leaned over the edge of his box and shouted, "That's a great play, Mr. Zangwill, that's a great play."

Israel Zangwill died on 1st August 1926 in Midhurst, West Sussex.

Index of Contents

Ad Unam

Take, Dear, my 'prentice songs,
And—since you cared for one,
"Blind Children"—let them all
Share in its blessedness,
Find shelter 'neath its name.
Are they not verily
Blind Children, one and all,
Wistfully haunted by
That unattainable
Glamorous sea of light
True poems float within?
Ah, could they hope to catch
One strange, rich gleam of it,
As they go haltingly,
Feeling their way to you,
Tapping their road to Truth,
Groping their path to God!

Sylva Poetarum

I

I lie within an ancient wood
That soothes the heart and stills the blood.
The leafy tongues in whispers sweet
Dead poets' syllables repeat.
Enchanted is each bird and tree,
The very air is poesy.
The shady places sacred lie
To solemn thought and vision high.
Here mossy oaks in sunshine sleep,
There bright, cool, living waters leap;
And, pav'd with clouds that swanlike pass,
Clear streams meander through the grass.
I hear from scented thicket float
Some plaintive songster's magic note.
For Winter's winds I take no fear,
The flowers blossom all the year.
The morning star or star of love
At pleasure palpitates above—
Fair Hesper, Queen of fond desire,
With tender rays of golden fire,
Or Lucifer, that, chasing night,
Throbs with serener, purer light.

Here Truth and Beauty find accord,
For Man reigns sole and Love is lord,
And Law is none save man's decree—
Yea, Man's creative fantasy;
And human eyes grow sweetly wet
To think that Life and Love have met.
Dissolving blend of dust and breath,
Man builds a world that mocks at death,
And, bubble in a sea of strife,
His life a dream, to dreams gives life.

II

What white-robed wanderers are these?
What white limbs flutter through the trees?
To yon clear fountains come the Nine,
And in this vale plays Proserpine.
(Beneath that beech lies Tityrus,
And yonder flutes Theocritus.)
Here Dryads dream and Naiads run,
And Satyrs frolic in the sun.
What loveliness gleams from afar?
Deep-bosomed Venus in her car,
Faring to where Adonis sleeps.
Adown the craggy mountain leaps
Diana of the silver bow,
As fierce as fire, as pure as snow.
Aurora spurs her horses white,
Athena walks, with eye of light,
Swift-drawn by peacocks Juno glides.
The flushed Olympians' earth-born brides
Appear—a bunch of living flowers
Soft-gleaming with celestial showers:
Zone-girdled maidens, very fair,
With ivory limbs and amber hair.
To beauty even gods must bow.
Apollo, sunshine on his brow,
And in his hand a shepherd's lyre,
Whose music charms the woodland quire,
Follows their train, and Oreads
Dance lightly down, while piping lads
Gaze amorous from thymy hills.
A radiant rout the pasture fills—
Ambrosia-breathing deities,
Unstained by human miseries.
No twilight mist, no subtle charm,
But noonday sunlight, bright and warm,
Or cloudless moonshine silver-fair,
And stainless depths of lucent air;
A level mead where you may smell

The amaranthine asphodel,
And hear with unperturbèd ear
A music joyous, high, and clear,
A pure, fresh fountain-leap of sound
Upwelling from a cool, sweet ground.
(No undertone of hidden pain
Like mournful plash of endless rain.)
Here earth is heaven, heaven earth,
And, of these twain resplendent birth,
Divinely perfect forms, serene
In calm white glory move between.

III

Ho, Ariel, daintiest of sprites!
Ho, gnomes and elves that frisk o' nights!
Immortals, merrily ye come
Duly at beat of Fancy's drum.
Here's tricksy Puck a-frolicking,
And fairies dancing in the ring.
Titania and Oberon
Greet Robin Hood and Little John.
Here's Rosalind in doublet straying,
Here's Perdita with blossoms playing.
The lion Una's lily hand
Is licking—ah! delightsome land,
Arcadia, Hesperides,
Or Arden, whose autochthones,
Because they never lived, live on,
And still shall live when we are gone.
Anon the cuckoo's "wandering voice"
Breaks out and bids the soul rejoice.
The lark pours forth his throbbing heart
With "unpremeditated art";
To heaven's gate, still singing, flies,
While marybuds "ope golden eyes."
The nightingale "on bloomy spray"
Warbles at silent eve his lay;
And when these sounds and sights oppress
The cabin'd soul with loveliness,
He fades "into the forest dim,"
The while his fading pinions skim
A cold wan water lorn of all
Save one wild swan's song, musical
With all the magic melodies
Of mermaids in enchanted seas,
Within whose haunting notes are set
Divine delight, divine regret.

IV

Ah, better this than earthly wood
That cramps the heart and chills the blood
With thoughts of never-ending strife
And sleepless Death pursuing Life;
Where aye the race is to the strong.
The olden magic in the song
Of birds, the charm of liquid notes
Down-raining from aerial throats
We cannot feel for stress of pain;
For on the sunshine is a stain,
And on the brow of Day a scar,
And o'er the Night an evil star.
The flowers all deflowered lie
Of that ethereal mystery
Which clung about a rose's scent,
And with its perfume subtly blent
A sense of something infinite,
Divinely sad, transcending wit.
The nymphs are gone, the fairies flown,
The olden Presences unknown,
The ancient gods forever fled,
The stars are silent overhead,
The music of the spheres is still,
The night is dark, the wind is chill,
The later gods have followed Pan,
And Man is left alone with Man.

At the Worst

"And Man is left alone with Man." 'Tis well!
The shapes that on the dusky background fell
From Man's bright soul are laid by morning's spell.
Why stay the Present 'gainst the Past to poise?
Man grown to Manhood spurns his childish toys
And wakes to grander fears and hopes and joys.
If aught is lost that we should long to keep,
'Tis Manhood's part to work and not to weep.
Old age comes on and everlasting sleep.
We are—whatever we have been before,
We have—whatever gold was in the ore;
God lives as much as in the days of yore,
In fires of human love and work and song,
In wells of human tears that pitying throng,
In thunder-clouds of human wrath at wrong.
The burning bush doth not the more consume,
New branches shoot where old no more illume,
Eternal splendour flames upon the gloom.

Though Hell and Heaven were a dream forgot,
And unregarded sacrifice our lot,
We serve God better, deeming He is not.
Perchance, O ye that toil on though forlorn,
By your souls' travail, your own noble scorn,
The very God ye crave is being born.
Not yet hath Man of faith and courage failed,
Albeit dazzled for a space and paled
By glimpse of Truth—God's awful face unveiled.
No change need be in all that we hold dear;
Love, Virtue, Knowledge, Beauty—all are here.
One Hope is gone but in its train one Fear.
The sea-wind blows as fresh; the ocean heaves
As blue and buoyant; Nature nowhere grieves;
As bright a green is on the forest leaves.
Larks sing and roses still are odorous,
Art, Poetry, and Music still for us,
And Woman just as fair and marvellous.
And if the earth with endless fray is rife,
Acknowledge in the universal strife
The zest of this, the seed of higher, life.
Evil is here? That's work for us to do.
The Old is dying? Let's beget the New.
And Death awaits us? Rest is but our due.

A London Hospital

I

O house of pain,
O'erbrooded by the wings of Death,
Who, starred with eyes, keeps watch on breath
And heart and brain.
'Mid greenery
O'ergloomed by London's sooty pall,
Weary with echoed wails thy wall
Stands drearily.
Towards it veers
A path which hope and fear have trod,
Whose stones might blossom like the sod
With rain of tears.
And London's veins
Branch out around—the poisoned courts,
The dusky roads where Sin resorts,
The dreary lanes.
And each so teems
With pain, with pain, thou seem'st their soul,
Their inmost heart through which to roll
Their anguished streams.

II

Lo, hither come
The wounded in th' eternal strife,
That makes yet mars our mortal life,
From street and slum.
The victor, Pain,
To glut his host retards day's flight
Until to long for truce of night
And sleep seems vain.

III

Here girls and boys
That know not life learn lore of death,
And man-like draw their latest breath
Amid their toys.
While battered men
Grow babes that hunger for the breast
Of mother earth, to sleep and rest
And pass from ken.

IV

When darkness falls
Without—for, every hour that dies,
The world grows dark to dying eyes
Within thy walls—
In pairs like doves,
'Mid flaring booths and bawling lungs,
The crowd, with talk in twenty tongues,
Lolls, laughs and loves.
But dying ears
Ignore the busy living street,
They hear the voices sad or sweet
Of buried years.

V

What realms are drawn
Within that narrow space! what styes,
Yet homes belov'd! what seas! what skies
At scarlet dawn!
What wingèd years
Flit by within each instant's thought,
With all the comedies they brought,

And all the tears!
What faces throng
From shadowland, that only live
In dying mem'ries, fugitive,
But sweet as song!

VI

No lovely thought
Dost thou express in stone; no will
Of artist, but the nobler thrill
By Pity wrought.
As thee we scan,
No radiant Grecian god we own,
Yet God made visible in stone,
The God in man.

VII

O house of pain,
O'erbrooded by the wings of Death,
Not He alone keeps watch on breath
And heart and brain.
Man's wisdom turns
Blind atoms' gall to healing wine,
Until the universe Divine
With mercy burns.

Epitome
Art thou of life, where meet the twain
High mysteries of love and pain
Eternally.

Blind Children

Laughing, the blind boys
Run round their college lawn,
Playing such games of buff
Over its dappled grass.
See the blind frolicsome
Girls in blue pinafores
Turning their skipping-ropes.
How full and rich a world
Theirs to inhabit is—
Sweet scent of grass and bloom,
Playmates' glad symphony,
Cool touch of western wind,

Sunshine's divine caress.
How should they know or feel
They are in darkness?
But, O the miracle!
If a Redeemer came,
Laid finger on their eyes—
One touch, and what a world,
New-born in loveliness!
Spaces of green and sky,
Hulls of white cloud adrift,
Ivy-grown college walls,
Shining loved faces.
What a dark world—who knows?—
Ours to inhabit is!
One touch, and what a strange
Glory might burst on us,
What a hid universe!
Do we sport carelessly,
Blindly upon the verge
Of an Apocalypse?

Faith and Words

What is Speech but just a net in which we seize
Some medusa, stickleback, or weed of fact,
While of ocean—left behind—the lees stream through?
Faiths as real if intangible as Song,
Feeling solid-based upon eternal rock,
Deep as Life and Death, and old as Truth and Time,
Do yet tremble when translated into Words.

Pastoral

A rich-toned landscape, touched with darkling gold
Of misty, throbbing cornfields, and with haze
Of softly-tinted hills and dreamy wold,
Lies warm with raiment of soft summer rays,
And in the magic air there lives a free
And subtle feeling of the distant sea.
The perfect day slips softly to its end,
The sunset paints the tender evening sky,
The shadows shroud the hills with gray, and lend
A softened touch of ancient mystery;
And ere the silent change of heaven's light
I feel the coming glory of the night.
Oh for the sacred, sweet responsive gaze
Of eyes divine with strange and yearning tears

To feel with me the beauty of our days,
The glorious sadness of our mortal years,
The noble misery of the spirit's strife,
The joy and splendour of the body's life!

A Song of Life

Praised be the lips of the Morn
For their musical message of Light,
For their bird-chanted burden of Song,
Praised be the young Earth re-born
For its freshness and glory and might,
And the thoughts of high, solemn delight
That at flash of its purity throng.
Praised be the lips of the Day
For their clarion call to the field
Where the Battle of Life must be fought.
Praised be the fire of the fray,
Where the soul is refined and annealed,
And the spirit heroic revealed,
And pure gold from base substances wrought.
Praised be the lips of the Night
For their murmurous message of Rest,
For their lullaby, motherly sweet.
Praised be the dreams of delight,
While tired Life is asleep in Love's nest,
And in harmony tender and blest
Heaven's calm and earth's loveliness meet.

Vision

The barge glided,
Rusty-hulled, yellow-sailed, on the green water,
From the dim lands and the child's dreams.
O the fresh romance and air of morning,
And the strange sweet tears!

The Argosy

With freight of golden memories
My galleon sails 'twixt wine-dark seas
And purple skies.
Her decks are crowned with visions fair
Of men and maids, and on the air
Rich music dies.

The odours of dim fairy soils
Enswathe her in sweet subtle coils
As on she steers
Through realms of Sleep and Poesie,
Soft lulled by far-off melody
From unborn years.
O memories impalpable!
O white sails' dream-like fall and swell,
And rise and dip!
Ah ghostly men and maidens fair!
Ah visionary sea and air!
O phantom ship!

Sunset

A touch of gold
Illumes the cold
And dreamy grace
Of heaven's face,
Then slowly dies
Like melody,
And darkness lies
On earth and sea—
'Tis sunset!
Good-bye to light
And visions clear,
For lo! the night,
The night is here.
But in the morn
Of sunny air,
When life is fair,
And love is born,
The glory dies
In youthful eyes,
Whose lids are wet
With wild regret—
'Tis sunset!
Good-bye to light
And visions dear.
Ah, weep! the night,
The night is here.

Alla Cantatrice

Waken, O songstress, enchantress, the springtide's romances,
Scatter the roses and lilies, the tulips and pansies.
Snatch the dull sceptre of Chronos, his iron laws scorning,

Marry all splendours and wonders of sunset and morning.
Marry all exquisite moments of passion and feeling—
Star-crowned heavens of Life, glory on glory revealing.
Summon the passionate years and the vanished places,
Laughter and sunlight give to the dear dead faces;
(Time yielding Music his dead, but, alas! soon recalling,
Leaving our arms vain-stretched and our tears swift falling.)
Cease, then, from rapture of song, mortal misery veiling,
Weave thee a girdle of Dirges, tumultuous, wailing,
Circled by which thou shalt type the deep soul of Existence,
Beauty at centre in holy, eternal persistence.
Sing till thy mournful music melts into mystical splendour,
Blending the chords of pain and delight into harmonies tender.
Waken, O songstress, enchantress, the spirit's romances,
Mother of tremulous dreams and of beautiful fancies.

A River Rondeau

How sweet to-night the river glides,
With restful swell of sleeping tides,
Beneath Diana's crescent-car!
Thick-gemmed with many a trembling star,
In sighing music on she slides.
Gray alders whisper on her sides,
Her bosom, lovely as a bride's,
Shows white with gleam of nenuphar,
How sweet to-night!
Ah, once to slip the lore that hides,
And wander from our purblind guides
To that young world which gleams afar,
Whose rivers dimpling Naiads are!
To be a Greek, while yon moon rides—
How sweet to-night!

A Spring Thought

Sweet Spring, thou comest girt with life and laughter,
Death shrinks before the sunlight of thy glances,
And at the music of thy Orphic harpings
The underworld yields up its buried blossoms.
And in our hearts thy melodies and odours
Can wake to passion'd life our olden glories.
Thou canst relume the glazèd eyes of Nature.
O Love, why is thy light gone out for ever?

Love and Death

Ah, weary days, how blank and drear,
When dust hid dust from thine embrace
And all the glory of the Year
Fled with the glory from her Face,
And memory was misery
And darkness fell on her and thee!
But with the days a second Birth
Of Love, instinct with purer grace,
Restores the glory to the Earth,
The olden glory to her Face,
And memory is harmony,
And Peace doth rest on her and thee.

Death's Transfiguration

We eat and drink and laugh and energize
In all the meanness of our daily lives,
And Death comes in our midst, a holy thing,
Like sacred night adorned with moon and stars,
And touches vulgar life with silver light.

Forever Young

Forever young, forever young!
Lo, Death hath stolen thee from Time,
And Love hath stolen thee from Death.
Forever thoughts of thee have clung
Round Nature—woodland air thy breath,
Thy voice the planetary chime.
Forever loved, seen everywhere,
In flowers thy lips, in stars thine eyes,
My soul grows royal by such grief.
Forever young and loved and fair,
With sunbeams, brooks and soft blue skies,
With bud and blossom, bird and leaf.

With the Dead

Light shadows fall across her grave,
A sweet wind stirs the flowered grass,
The song-girt branches slowly wave,
The solemn moments softly pass.
The afternoon draws quiet breath

At pause between the eve and morn,
And from the sacred place of Death
The holy thoughts of Life are born.
I fret not at the will of doom;
Her soul and mine are not apart.
Dear violets upon her tomb,
Ye blossom in my heart.

The Bridge

Death is no kingdom dark and dreary,
For thou art there.
Sunnily flows the Stygian river
Through lucent air.
Ever with sacred joy I see thee
And awed delight.
What can divide us, friend and lover,
Who in thy flight
Madest as one the mystic regions
Time severeth,
Leaving a track of light refulgent
'Twixt Life and Death!

Perspective

My feet on the ball of St. Peter's,
My head in the radiant skies,
I see the Eternal City
Shrunk to an ant-heap's size:
Re-sucked to eternal forest,
Absorbed in the greenness around.
O pother of Black ants and White ants,
Contending upon your mound!
The domes are dwindled to mushrooms,
The towers are sunk to stones,
Live Rome and its ruins are equal,
The dog and the lion's bones.
Is this the world's great wonder?
To this do all roads lead?
Here forged the Church's thunder?
Here cast the Church's creed?
O pitiful breed of mortals,
O spawn of a teeming womb,
What Brobdingnagian boasting,
What Liliputian doom!
But sudden a thought brings comfort—
Man's littleness thus I can scan,

Because I am high on St. Peter's,
Upborne by the greatness of man!

Rosalind reading an Old Romance.
I watch her dainty rosebud mouth,
That trembles with the exquisite
And wondrous tide that steals from it
Of song, resplendent of the South;
While o'er her April countenance,
The music of the quaint romance,
The sweeter for a sense of pain,
Sends sun and shade and, lost in dream,
Her sweet eyes softly flash and gleam
With golden smiles and diamond rain.

To a Pretty Girl

Silly girl! Yet morning lies
In the candour of your eyes,
And you turn your creamy neck,
Which the stray curl-shadows fleck,
Far more wisely than you guess,
Spite your not unconscious dress.
In the curving of your lips
Sages' cunning finds eclipse,
For the gleam of laughing teeth
Is the force that works beneath,
And the warmth of your white hand
Needs a God to understand.
Yea, the stars are not so high
As your body's mystery,
And the sea is not so deep
As the soul in you asleep.

Chastity

In stainless purity calm Nature lies.
The snow that seems so chill without keeps warm
The inward breast and beautifies the earth
With noble floriage. Even so the soul
In sacramental purity arrayed,
Blossoms.

Helena: An Early Portrait

Strange earnest glance that boldly looks ahead,
Illuminate with false prophetic fire,
Unconscious of the blankness of the days
When eyes grow dim with sudden unsought tears.
To Helena—later.
We need not seek to know
What deeds of evil men defile this earth,
Supremely coarse, ineffably unclean.
We need not mark the roar
Of mirth obscene, it is enough to know
That thou art pure and good,
That thou art kind and true.
Follow thy music, bear thy goodness high
Through all the subterrene of human lot
And trust the Purpose, though it seems so void,
A Light to others, dark unto thyself.

Psychology

He and she met almost daily,
Parting then to analyze
In their diaries each the other,
Psychologically wise.
Now the dust is on their eyes.

Maligned

Others, Kitty, do you wrong,
Rating you not worth a song.
For, said they, you do but jest
With the hearts that love you best.
I, poor poet, disagree:
You were worth a song to me.

Winter

I wandered through the wintry wood,
No buds to peep, no birds to sing;
Sudden, amid my drearihood,
I turned mine eyes and saw the Spring—
'Twas you!
You gleamed across the snowy waste
With dancing step and sunny hair.
You passed me by in careless haste.
My heart is ice, my boughs are bare—

Adieu!

The sunshine road and pavement floods,
Folk gaily come and go,
And in my frozen soul Love buds
At last above the snow.
Upon the sunbeams of the Strand
I see her image float,
Her dancing eyes, her little hand,
Her dainty petticoat.
And then I see but mist above,
Remembering forlorn,
The sweet Spring day will die; her love
For me will ne'er be born.

If Love be but a bubble,
Blown from the pipe of Life,
That bursts and leaves but trouble
And weariness and strife,
Then who would cares redouble
And leave his years as stubble
And sorrow take to wife?
If Love be but a bubble
Blown from the pipe of Life.
If Love be but a bubble
Blown from the pipe of years,
Its beauty is but double
That it is built of tears,
And for its tender trouble
I'd leave my life as stubble
And pluck my ripest ears,
Though Love be but a bubble
Blown from the pipe of years.

For this the ancient stars were hurled
And monsters mixed in oozy strife.
These were the birth-pangs of the world,
That Love might come to life.

The Sign-post

"To Heaven," "To Hell," so said the guiding fingers.
I looked to right, to left, around, above:
The self-same path it was to which both pointed;
Then saw I that the road was Sexual Love.

A Stage Illusion

The torches flare, the music falls,
The dancers circle to and fro;
Within her kinsmen's festive halls
I stand, a masked and hated foe.
I seek her ardent Southern glance,
Her beauty burns my blood to wine—
But to the rhythm of the dance
My heartstrings wail: "She is not mine;
Ah, never mine."
The orchard blooms, the moon is bright,
As with sweet looks and soft replies
The spirit of the Southern night
Draws up my soul through ears and eyes.
And in my heart and in my brain
There throbs in music argentine
One blissful passionate refrain,
"She loves thee, loves thee—she is thine;
Forever thine."
Within the dusky tomb I lie,
Yet sweet the charnel house's breath,
For she is nigh, my love is nigh—
Ah God, would this indeed were death!
Vain wish—mad plaudits mock my ears
And wake me from the dream divine,
And I—poor mummer—through my tears
Remember that she is not mine;
Ah, never mine.

Love's Prayer

Though thy starlike spirit shine
O'er the earthliness of mine,
Let Love only be my plea,
Love me but for loving thee.

Love and Letters

Of Love so often did I sing
In literary woe,
Avengeress, you came to bring
The cruel, real blow.
But still the Muse you cannot best,
Your rival bides her time,
Then soothes the pain within my breast
By putting it in rhyme.

Inexhaustible

Of woman and wine, of woods and spring,
And all fair things that be,
The poets have sung of everything:
What is there left for me?
Why, songs of thee.

Song

Forgive me if when meadows blow
And lanes are all a-trill with song,
And hedges gleam with scented snow,
And visions fair on mortals throng—
Forgive me, of thy gentle grace,
If I can find 'mid sweets so choice
No fairer vision than thy face,
No dearer music than thy voice.
Forgive me if when bleak rain drips,
And mist obscures the wintry skies,
I find June's roses on thy lips,
June's heaven in thy radiant eyes.
So craving skies for ever blue,
And roses ever at my door,
Forgive me if I ask for you,
For I love much—and more and more.

A Pastel

Child or woman, as you please,
Gravely young or gaily old,
Muse to fire and minx to tease,
Loving, yet how pure and cold!

Diana with a colour-box,
Scorning all the sex of man,
Sweetly-glancing Paradox,
Angel and Bohemian.
Wild-bird caged in city grim,
Drooping sans the fevered streets,
Head of logic, heart of whim,
Strong-willed, weak-willed, colds and heats.
Box of melodies at strife,
Pagan, Christian, humble, vain,
Craving death—and fuller life:
Paris—or Siena's fane.
Purse-forgetting business-man,
Counting gain on fingers slim,
Socialist the world to scan
Through the tears that doubly dim.
Rosy revolutionist,
Preaching loud the reign of Peace,
While her pretty lips unkist
Wars of man and man increase.
Raise me from the arid dust,
Kindle faiths and dreams forgone,
Shining eyes of love and trust,
Breast to rest a life upon!

Ballade of a Curious Couple

Rough-knobbed and gnarl'd and with muddy splashes,
And dabs of green from the grassy clay,
Where the garish restaurant's gas-light flashes,
It leans in nonchalant lounging way
Beside a delicate dream in gray.
They look like giant at rest with doll,
Together tired at the close of day—
The walking-stick and the parasol.
With night and cookery gently clashes
That dainty sunshade, suggesting play
Of light and shadow and drooping lashes,
And leaves sun-glinted and ocean spray,
And more poetical things than they.
While of everything that is fou and folle
In reckless duet they chant the lay—
The walking-stick and the parasol.
The sunset's beautiful colour-dashes
Have faded out to the final ray,
The sky that glowed is in cold gray ashes,
Felicity never arrives to stay.
But will its memory die away?
They cannot talk like your pretty Poll,

Or else I wonder what they would say—
The walking-stick and the parasol.

Envoy

Princess of all that is bright and gay,
Perhaps we know, though demure they loll,
If they flirted under the sky of May—
The walking-stick and the parasol.

May

My darling shines,
All lyric lines,
And singing motions,
With wavering gleams
Of wistful dreams
And dim devotions.
Such nameless grace
Across her face
Evasive trembles;
Whate'er is fair
In earth or air
In her assembles.
Her dancing eyes
Outdo the skies
For rays that hover;
Such living light
The orbs of night
Nor day discover.
Thus in all things
Her image swings,
And sings and dances.
Love her, have all!
How blest the thrall
Who serves her glances!

Feminine Theology

Immortal was her soul, she said!
I inly smiled to think of all
The doubts by her unknown, unread,
Who still believed in Adam's fall,
Nor knew that good men question Paul.
Dogmatic puss! To settle so
What saints and sages longed to know,
And none had whispered from the dead!

Immortal was her soul, she knew!
Rose lips exposed her ignorance
Of any other point of view
With such bewitching arrogance,
Her eye shot such a spiritual glance,
That I, half dazzled by the flash
Of sunlight stored beneath her lash,
Began to think that mine was too.

Street Wanderers

Dear child, as mid the crowd we stand,
Where noisy barrows shine,
I love to feel your little hand
Slip gently into mine.
Then of a sudden to recall,
As though I saw a star,
What is, dear child, the best of all,
That you a woman are.

Aspiration

O for the simpler life,
For tents and starry skies,
And the dreams that brood and dance
In Una's eyes!
O for the peace of faith,
If not in God above,
Then at least in life and work,
Through Una's love!

Blind Fools

I would you were not pretty!
Blind fools will always say,
My love is but a petty
Desire for earthly clay.
Your beauty but a torch is
To show your lovelier soul.
No empty temple's porch is
My pilgrimage's goal!
Yet sans your outer graces,
Should I have paused to find
The inner holy places?
The fools are not so blind!

Expectation

All day I had thought of the night,
Of the night when she would come;
Her name was a pulse of delight
At my heart, though my lips were dumb.
My guests poured merrily in;
I greeted I know not whom,
As, framed in the friendly din,
I stood in an empty room.
There was many a luring face
A painter or poet would prize;
I only thought of the grace
Of her faraway haunting eyes.
There's a rustle within the hall,
And the long suspense is past:
She is coming, the crown of all—
She is coming, my own at last.
I smile, shake her hand, and speak
Some cold conversational word;
Though I feel her breath on my cheek,
My pulse is all unstirred.
At her kiss my horizon gray
Should flame as the sun-fired West;
Indifferent, I turn away
And talk to another guest.

A Summer Song

Far better than to build the rhyme
Of empty words it is to hold
Your hand beneath a sky of gold
At sunset in the summer time.
Far sweeter thus to kiss your eyes
And take life's fulness at the flood
Than, lying stranded in the mud,
To weave phantasmal melodies.
To do is higher than to dream,
To feel is truer than to think,
And wiser at your lips to drink
Than at the pale Pierian stream.
Yet as this lovely summer-time
Your sweetness in my arms I hold,
I feel my kisses growing cold,
And all things turning into rhyme.

Love's Labour Lost

I sent up my thoughts like roses
To climb to the casement of Love,
But no face ever shone in the darkness,
No whisper e'er beckoned above.
And now that the casement stands open,
And now that the door stands wide,
'Tis no longer a man, warm and breathing,
But a shadow that flits outside.

Realization

When you were but a dream
Such things befell,
So bitter, it might seem
I lived in hell.
But never heaven's gleam
Quite left my cell;
'Twas but an evil dream
To you to tell.
Now that in you my dream
Grows visible,
I crawl from Stygian stream
Too tired to tell.

Two Kinds of Love

Two kinds of Love, the one of moonlight wan,
Fretted with fluttering fevers, querulous,
And one that is as sunshine, sweet and plain,
Sea-breezes keen and all the buoyant day.

To a Dear Inconstant

As still amid the flux of things
And purposeless gray happenings
Some force subsists that makes for Beauty,
And something through the chaos sings;
So 'mid your fevered flutterings,
Or airy flights on proud-poised wings,
Some wistful instinct gropes for Duty,
And still o'er all your vagrom moods

Love, like a clouded heaven, broods.
Dear, trust the still, small voice; distrust
The fawning court of lesser selves,
The tricksy swarm of sprites and elves,
Informed with sly, usurping lust
To drag the central "you" to dust,
And render mute the sovereign "must"
That sends them scurrying to their delves.
Let their gay friskings serve to grace thy reign,
But be thou Queen by work and love and pain.

Sundered

Once between us the Atlantic,
Yet I felt your hand in mine;
Now I feel your hand in mine,
Yet between us the Atlantic.

Wasted

You, whose Face should have witched a poet
From sunless gloom to a deathless song,
Linked to your love, to your mere mate mated,
To one instead of the world belong.

Lost

Quaintly she lies in the light,
Stirless her passionate breath,
Decked in her wedding robes white,
Decked in the glory of Death,
Lost, ever lost unto me.
Dumbstruck in trying to speak
Word that would make her a wife.
Roses have fled from her cheek,
Roses have fled from my life:
Lost, ever lost unto me.
Lover was I, now forlorn,
Stony and still lieth she—
Masters, 'tis just that I mourn.
Ask ye why weepeth thus He—
"Lost, ever lost unto me?"
He was to wed her to-day,
False, she was false unto me.
He is a villain, I say—

Villain, but she could not see:
Lost, ever lost unto me.
Warning to her gave I none,
Glad to her wedding I hied.
Gloating o'er vengeance begun,
Sweet'ning my years—but she died:
Lost, ever lost unto me.

Après

Burning my songs, "There's naught to follow;
All is over for me," I said.
"Women are false and the world is hollow;
Better far to be lying dead."
Long was the night, but the morn did follow,
Then a bitterer truth I learnt:
"Women are false and the world is hollow;"
True, most true—but my songs are burnt.

Asti Spumante

Its pop excites my fellow-diners' glances
With images of reckless revelry.
Within a broad-brimmed glass it froths and dances,
Showy as Moët and as cheap as tea.
I pass the bottle to my silent neighbour,
He smacks his lips and spouts of mother Earth,
The ripe grape's tang and Nature's tropic labour,
Her tameless travail of eternal birth.
I pass the bottle to the man loquacious,
The tragic bard of Asti he recalls,
And Pisa's Campo Santo, white and spacious,
With that quaint fresco on the ancient walls:
The Vintage—grapes and grapes in purple splendour;
Green-kirtled gleaners; feet in vats deep-sunk;
O'erbrimming baskets borne by maidens slender,
And in a corner Noah lying drunk.
Ah yes, the Asti brings them pleasant fancies,
For me alone it works a miracle.
My childhood with its glamorous romances
Lies in a drop of that cheap Muscatel.
One sip—and fled the public foreign table,
Trust, innocence and wonder, all are mine!
For Asti, though Spumante, is unable
To hide relationship to raisin-wine.
The raisin-wine of ceremonies holy,
Wherein—to fête old Pharaoh's overthrow—

We dipped unleavened bread: the East moves slowly,
'Twas only some three thousand years ago.
O witching night when Earth was near to Heaven,
O blessedness to be a little Jew!
Where lay the magic in not eating leaven?
And how was Noah aped on raisin-brew?
I know not, but by Asti re-created,
All dewy-fresh the young enchantments rise,
And I forget that I am old and sated,
Lonely, and stained of soul, and worldly-wise.
Prate on, O friends, of Nature, Art and Dante,
Nor note my tears are weakening the wine
Your world is stale as yesterday's Spumante,
My Ghetto sparkles youthfully divine.

Dead Memories

Lately an elderly Frenchwoman
Showed me a dress with embroidery,
Delicate, worn by her grandmother
Once at the Court of Napoleon.
Instantly flashed the great Corsican
Duskily bright on my memory,
Crumbled to dust with his dynasty
Long ere the dainty embroidery.
Also I strove to resuscitate
All those gay splendours the grandmother
Moved amid, but unsuccessfully,
Knowing so little of History.

A Song of Subscriptions

In ancient years the chevaliers
Rode out on schemes quixotic,
With hand on blade, e'er ready laid,
To draw at deeds despotic.
But each true knight still aids the Right,
However cynics mock it.
To aid Love's law we moderns draw—
The money from our pocket.
In early ages the peering sages
Sought long that great tradition,
The chymic stone, and, were it known,
It were a great magician.
But—far above—warm human Love
Makes roses out of nettles—
To Thought and Light and Truth and Right

Transmutes the baser metals.

Country Holiday Fund

The cry of the children is answered
In so far as an answer may be;
Their laughter is heard in the woodlands
And down by the sea.
With all that is young they are frisking—
The fawn and the lamb and the bee.
They are nesting divine recollections
For the drearisome days that shall come—
Green pastures, sweet haystacks and roses
Shall flash on the slum,
Bird-music, the song of the waters,
Shall throb in machinery's thrum.
But the toil-wearied mothers whose foreheads
Are aching in fœtid town-air,
Whose souls are too sad for expectance,
Too dulled for despair,
The saints of the needle and wash-tub,
Their cry—is it heard anywhere?

The Peace Conference

(July, 1890)

Upon War's shield and shadowed by his sword,
Behold the pigmies who dare dream to slay
The giant, who, although he doze to-day,
To-morrow shall new-cram his gorge abhorred.
Long yet his blood-libation shall be poured!
Long yet the peoples shall acclaim his sway!
Our earth cools faster than the ancient zest
Of blood, the dull hereditary hate,
The prejudices inarticulate,
The greed and jealousy that unexprest
Still smoulder in the patriotic breast
And must upflame in ire inveterate.
Yet dreams are half-deeds, and this solid world
Is built on visions; wherefore let no scorn
Greet those who in the midnight grope for morn,
And dream that War's red banner shall be furled,
And War's foul reek of smoke and blood be curled
No more about an earth renewed, re-born.

A Political Character

In him the elements are strangely blent—
Two consciences he hath, two hearts, two souls,
On double wrongs and errors he is bent,
And ne'er appears except in dual rôles.
He hears both sides, but 'tis with different ears;
Sees both sides of the shield—with different eyes;
Between two Rights with nice precision steers,
This double-headed King of Compromise.
Not his to hold the scales of Life and Death—
Not his, this nebulous invertebrate,
Who heeds and scorns at once the vulgar breath,
Nor knows the fixity which stamps the great.
The kingly souls with instinct for the Right,
Vibrant to conscience and her trumpet-call,
With clarity of vision, inward light,
And strength to follow out their thought through all.

In Mentone

An Afric lion in a cage,
Worn dumb with woe and futile rage,
His forest eye-sight dimmed with age,
Grim-couchant on his balcony,
He turns his back to sun and sea,
And scowls upon humanity.
Swift-thunder past his prison doors
To Monte Carlo's gala shores
The motors of his conquerors.
The flaunting females throned elate
Make bitterer his kindred's fate,
He blinks and mourns his buried mate.
Oom Paul, believing over-much,
Your faith in God and man was such
You dared to put it to the touch!
And so you finish far from home,
Your Temple split from floor to dome,
Your Empire smashed like yon white foam.
But yet you chew no novel crust—
Who has not staked his dreams? What trust
Has Fate not smitten to the dust?
One trusts in Love. Friend, keep aloof!
Of moonbeams weave both warp and woof,
Put nothing to the solid proof.
One trusts in Fame. Already surge
Oblivion's waters. What! Emerge?
Your juniors chant your funeral dirge.

One trusts in Truth. Ay, shout her praise,
But march not to her Marseillaise—
A crown of thorns her only bays!
One trusts in Justice. Cursèd Jew
To put our France in such a stew!
Your champion chokes—and so may you!
Take, Paul, a fellow-exile's hand,
I, too, have lost my fairyland,
I, too, have waked—to understand.

To Joseph Jacobs

(Prefaced to his edition of "Barlaam and Josaphat," 1895)

O friend, who sittest young yet wise
Beneath the Bô-tree's shade,
Confronting life with kindly eyes,
A scholar unafraid
To follow thought to any sea
Or back to any fount,
'Tis modern morals that to me
From thy excursions mount.
Was Barlaam one with Josaphat,
And Buddha likewise each?
What better parable than that
The unity to preach—
The simple brotherhood of souls
That seek the highest good;
He who in kingly chariot rolls,
Or wears the hermit's hood!
The Church mistook? These heathens once
Among her saints to range!
That deed of some diviner dunce
Our wisdom would not change.
For Culture's Pantheon they grace
In catholic array.
Each Saint hath had his hour and place,
But now 'tis All Saints' Day.

The Æsthete's Damnation

On earth he long had bloomed
With bland and airy phrases.
To Hell his soul was doomed—
At once he sang its praises.
"Such subtle sinuous flare,
Such restful red unrest,

Half shadow and half glare,
Like Rembrandt at his best."
The imps heaped high the coal,
The bellows 'gan to blow,
Cried out the burning soul:
"Quite Fra Angelico!
"What decorative grace
In flames that twist and twine!
How they light the Devil's face
And make it all divine!
"What life-enhancing zest
In every living curve,
O golden urns o' the blest,
I thrill in every nerve!
"And while the light is ruddy,
And while my zeal is hot,
Oh what a chance to study
My Dante on the spot!"
Then Satan grimly swore:
"I damn you up to heaven,
Where you'll find life a bore,
And a day as long as seven.
"Where the souls sit round and purr
O'er each soporific blessing,
Where the music is amateur,
And the art is life-depressing."

Why Do We Live?

First self:
Well, alter ego, Time has trudged
Once more his annual circuit, neighbour.

Second self:
And once again, friend, we're adjudged
Twelve months' hard labour.

First self:
With Death as an alternative.

Second self:
To Mercy's side there's some inclining.

First self:
Then why continue we to live,
Though always whining?

Second self:
Because we've got so used to both!

To live and whine preceded long-clothes.
For suicide mankind is loth:
'Tis thought a wrong close.

First self:
Bah! Sift it in impartial sieve
Why men such pains themselves are giving.

Second self:
I know not. Most men seem to live
To get a living.

First self:
Upon itself this answer twists,
The question still remains a vexed one.

Second self:
Each generation but exists
To get the next one.

First self:
Pray drop this tone of de'il-may-care,
And please return a serious answer
To why the nations keep up their
Eternal dance, sir?

Second self:
We live to fight, the preachers cry,
The evil in us—brief, the Devil.
Our bodies battlefields supply
For contests civil.

First self:
Let canting preachers think me bold,
I can't accept their explanation
That we exist to give the Old
'Un occupation.

Second self:
Nor I. We know we live. That's sure.
With this one fact assertion's pow'r ends,
One theory though I think secure—
'Tis not for our ends.

First self:
The "why" cannot be understood
Except by transient gleams and flashes.
So let's muse less and do more good
Before we're ashes.
For lo! night comes when none can work.
Work while 'tis day, my puling brother.

"Why do we live?" let's henceforth shirk.

Second self:
Well, ask another.

The Prophet's Message

They called him Prophet, Seer and Sage,
The Light, the Teacher of the Age.
Obscure too long, he shone at length:
The millions leaned upon his strength.
One summer morn self-slain he died,
They found this Message at his side:
"I die because my soul is bare
Of faith and all except despair."

In the Morgue

The sunbeams streamed without,
The wind-tossed boughs made riot;
A man on boards laid out
Reposed in waxen quiet.
A poet paused to view
The corpse, and wept, poor poet:
"I am more dead than you,
Because, alas, I know it!"

Night Mood

My mind is as a sea of shudd'ring pines
At thick o' night when all's asleep but wind—
Wind blindly groping in the heavy darkness—
And formless shapes crowd round their mother Night,
And all the moonless, starless horror seems
Of old and changeless, hopeless, everlasting.
Terror in Darkness.
I feel the breath of midnight,
As of some uncouth creature, panting quick
At tension for a spring, awaiting which
I live but in the pulses of my heart.
At Dead o' Night.
And I looked up and lo! the Night was dead,
Its myriad eyes closed,
Its breath still.
And the dull cloudy shroud

Hung movelessly around it.
I was alive, but the Night was dead.
I could not die with the tired Night.

Hopeless

Alone until I die—alone, alone,
Abhorring mine own self and other men.
The sunlight casts Death's shadow and not mine;
With Death's dread shadow ever do I walk.
I see Him not but feel his icy air.
Sometimes his sobs do hurtle in mine ear,
His heart doth break for anguish of his deeds.

The Sign

The man peers silently into the dim
Blank eyes of the dead universe with tears,
Because there is no sign shown unto him
Save memories of their smile in childish years.

Dream-Picture

And dead men singing
Rowed o'er the ferry,
And the moonlight glistened
On faces merry.
And in a twinkling
The rowers vanished,
The water plashless,
The voices banished,
But the oars kept glancing
And the boat advancing.

To the Blessèd Christ

O blessèd Christ, that foundest death
When life was fire and tears,
Not drawing on a sluggish breath
Through apathetic years!
Still, still about Thy forehead gleams
The light we know Thee by.
O blessèd Christ, to die for dreams

Nor know that dreams would die!

Incarnation

O God, if Thou indeed didst take
Our feeble human form,
A human heart to ache and break,
A brow to meet the storm.
If Thou indeed hast drunk our cup,
And known the doom of Right,
A gentler God went surely up
To re-assume His might.

Hinc Illæ Lachrymæ

Not hence, O Earth, the saddest tears we weep—
That we are puny creatures of thy crust,
And swift revert to our parental dust,
Which breeds from e'en the ashes of our sleep;
Nor that the span of time 'tis ours to creep
Above our graves is darkened by distrust
And marred by sordid cares and pangs unjust,
Not from our pain the deepest tears upleap.
But hence our tears—that through the mists of youth
There gleams a golden world of miracle
Which, even when its glamour fades and ruth
Has dispossessed our sense that all is well,
Still stirs by lovely face or lofty truth
Some dream of Beauty unpossessable.

Vanitas Vanitatum

A rich voluptuous languor of dim pain,
A dreamy sense of passionate regret,
Delicious tears and some sweet, sad refrain,
Some throbbing, vague and tender canzonet,
That mourns for life so real and so vain,
Wherein we glory while our eyes are wet.

Summer Evening Rain in London

Soft lambent rain that dims the starlit air,
A trembling, misty gleam from twinkling lights;

A touch of freshness, vague and cool and fair,
Imblent with that vast sadness which is Night's:
Stern London's face, suffused with tender tears,
As if with thought of all the vanished years.

Dreams

I craved for flash of eye and sword,
I dreamt of love and glory,
And Fate—who sends dreams their award—
Unfolds like changeless coils of cord
Life's long slow sordid story.

Voiceless

No toil I'd count, no theft of time,
No wound unstaunched, no sin unshriven,
If only from the sweat and slime
Some wingèd lyric rose to heaven.
But ah for me no song redeems,
My cross a fardel but of faggots;
My tears have caught no rainbow gleams,
And in the slime lo! eyeless maggots!

The Cynic

When I and my cynical note are dead,
Dead as my heart is now,
And sneer-writhen lips shall their last have said,
Their au diable of wearihead,
Then fresh young life shall aspire and vow
And light shall gleam in eye and brow,
And joy upleap and passion burn,
Though my heart of dust to the dust return.
When I and my cry of revolt are dead,
Dead as my palsied brain,
My wisdom must to the winds be shed:
I die—as I lived—in vain.
Fresh hearts shall swell with the same sweet lies,
Old visions be mirrored in youthful eyes,
The sun shall kindle the morning sea,
When God's gag lies on the mouth of me.

At the Zoo

The sky is gray with rain that will not fall,
The clayey paths are oozing ghostly mist.
Reeking with sadness immemorial,
The gray earth saps the courage to exist.
Poor tropic creatures, penned in northern land,
I, too, desire the sun and am a slave.
My heart is with you, and I understand
The lion turning in his living grave.

Despair and Hope

Despair of all, and hope for none!
We are unclean beneath the sun.
Foul vapours cling to all that's high,
Notes jar in every harmony.
We tame our flights to lower goals,
Mean deeds defile the purest souls.
Trust nothing—this alone is sure:
We pass, and nothing will endure.
For all men hope, despair of none!
Foul vapours flee, the golden sun
The darkest puddles draws on high
To paint the sky with harmony.
So Love shall lift to higher goals
The lowest lives, the darkest souls.
Rejoice we then, of one thing sure:
We pass, but deeds of love endure.

The Sense of Justice

Who armed us with the righteous meting-rod
By which our trust in heavenly love grows dim?
The fact that you and I despair of God
Is common ground for hope and faith in Him.

A Winter Morning's Mood

Heart-sick I step from out the dusky hall . . .
God! What a burst of brightness all adorning!
Blue, frosty sky, still streets grown magical
Beneath the sacred splendour of the morning.
Strange music swells, dead faces flash and gleam,
God's face resurges in the luminous glory.

God's love a moment seems no hopeless dream,
Nor Immortality an old wives' story.

In The City

Sudden amid the slush and rain,
I know not how, I know not why,
A rose unfolds within my brain,
And all the world is at July.
A trumpet sounds, green surges splash,
And daffodillies dance i' the sun;
Through tears fair pictures flit and flash
Upon the City's background dun.
Women are true and men are good,
Concord sleeps at the heart of strife.
How sweet is human brotherhood,
And all the common daily life!

Sic Transit

Dreamy sound of rain at dying summer eve,
Dewy sight of grass at living summer morn,
Drowsy scent of rose at sleeping summer noon,
Ye to me are sweet as life, as death forlorn.
Through my tears I feel your loveliness divine,
For your freshness or your sweetness seems to blend
With diviner dawns and sunsets soul-create,
Unalloyed with our inevitable end.

"Non Omnis Moriar"

"Immortal as the Gods!" But they
Half grudge the boon they share and give.
"I shall not wholly die," you say,
But neither did I wholly live.

Invocation

O come, thou starry-eyed rich summer night
Voluptuous, and rain soft feathery rest
Upon the furrowed summits of the hills,
And fill the air with delicate scents and sounds,
Flying with olden mem'ries in their train.

So the sad earth shall tremble passionate
Under the melting kisses of the moon,
And, glad as fair, send up her fragrant soul
In silvern swoon of languishing delight.

Palingenesis

No care for beauty, joy in skies or woods,
That lived in silence round me, but soft touch
Of Death's persuasive hand. I was so young.
My watch-dog Reason kept so fierce a ward
Against the thieves and beggars of the heart,
The hungry dreams, the faiths that cry for food,
The desp'rate hopes that force all Logic's locks
(Ah me, were not Unreason wiser far?)
Methought experience was a scroll unrolled
And Life was but re-thumbing it till Death,
For I had flown through every zone of Thought
And reached the frigid shores of nothingness,
And overbrooding dusk where is no dream
Of beauty, joy in woods or skies, but touch
Of Death's persuasive hand. Lo, there I dwelt
How long I know not but in Polar night.
At last a shiver in the sleeping leaves
That lived in silence round me, purple light,
Sweet tremors in the air, vague pulsing sounds,
Stirrings and echoes of divine delight,
Bursts of bird-music, flush of panting souls
Of roses, leapings of the dancing heart,
And life a song, an empyrean chant
Of sunrise, splendour, glory, beauty, force,
Inwove with tender dreams and blown upon
By breath of Passion from the centuries,
Immortal airs from realms of old Romance,
And life re-born at radiant dawn of Love.

"Might is Right"

So Might is Right, you say; I fight in vain
To make a transcendental justice reign.
Works thus the world? No more, my soul, be numb,
For might is right until a mightier come.

The Fight with Evil

O youth of the world, come again
And exchange our sluggish sigh
For the rage of a wild white main
That pants and tugs at its chain
And leaps at the throat of the sky.

A Working Philosophy

The solar system turns without thine aid.
Live, die! The universe is not afraid.
What is is right! If aught seems wrong below,
Then wrong it is—of thee to leave it so.
Then wrong it first becomes for human thought,
Which else would die of dieting on naught.
Tied down by race and sex and creed and station,
Go, learn to find thy strength in limitation,
To do the little goal that comes to hand,
Content to love and not to understand;
Faithful to friends and country, work and dreams,
Knowing the Real is the thing that seems.
While reverencing every nobleness,
In whatsoever tongue, or shape, or dress,
Speak out the word that to thy soul seems right,
Strike out thy path by individual light;
'Tis contradictory rays that give the white.

A Singer to His Song

O wingèd poem that unsought
Hast broke the shell of worldly thought,
Go—fashioned perfect at thy birth,
Unlike the nestlings of the earth—
Forth-fluttering go with swelling throat,
On waves of thine own music float
To sunless regions, there to rest
And nestle in Man's icy breast,
And warm it with celestial fire,
And wake his frozen heart's desire
For Love and Beauty, Good and Truth
And all the sacred dreams of Youth.
Dear offspring of the wedded might,
Of human sorrow and delight,
Ere thou couldst soar on Helicon,
To thy creation there had gone
My spirit's every element
With every sensuous image blent.
Fair Nature's scents and sounds and sights,

The magic of her days and nights,
Her harmonies of hue and form,
Her fiery rhapsodies of storm,
The fragrant freshness of her Springs,
Her warm, voluptuous blossomings,
The wail of orphan winds forlorn,
The purple pageantry of morn,
The rich-stained windows of the West,
The tossing ocean's snowy crest,
The radiance of Woman's eyes
Where Being's secret lives and dies,
Dim haunting peals of plaintive rhymes
Like sunken cities' far-off chimes,
With solemn organ-rolls and swells
Of long sonorous syllables,
Glad memories with gray alloyed,
All I have suffered or enjoyed,
From splendours of my childhood's dawn
With seraph-shapes by Fancy drawn,
To glooms and grandeurs of the man
Astray in paths without a plan;
My lusts, my loves, my hates, my fears,
My sighs and laughter, smiles and tears,
In thee, in thee they live once more,
But strangely nobler than before.
For thou art touched with sacred gleams,
The essence of divinest dreams,
The mystic flash that flees control,
The life of life, the soul of soul.
And as a mother dimly feels,
Whilst down her cheek soft moisture steals,
Her infant moving in her womb,
So I amid Life's fret and fume
Have joyed to feel thy Presence sweet,
Full knowing thou, yet incomplete,
Must shape thyself to symmetry
Before thou couldst be born to me—
Have felt the chords of bliss and pain
Vibrating vaguely in my brain
With mystic, mournful melody
Far sweeter than all minstrelsy
Wherewith an earthly artist stirs
Low-breathing lutes and dulcimers.
Go, lyric bird! Thy lovely song
Unfaltering through Time prolong.
Yet, songster mine, I crave for thee
No empty immortality,
That thou within a gilded cage
Make music for a pleasured age.
Sing on till Love and Truth be dead,
Sing on till Innocence be fled;

Then share of fairer things the lot:
Die, perish, vanish, be forgot.

Morning Piece

(Sea of Marmora, 1897)

A scarlet glory burned fantastically splendid
In the sky of dawn,
Like a vision of the Apocalypse.
The sea stretched blue and stainless,
The wind blew fresh across the great spaces.
The white ship glided across the morning waters
Like a living thing rejoicing in its grace.
A sense of largeness, freedom, purity, infinity,
Breathed from all things.
And, huddled like animals in the hold of the ship,
And packed on the fore-deck,
And swarming on the hatches,
And coiled in the ropes,
And seething beneath the awnings,
Hundreds and hundreds of Greek refugees
In their grimy clothes
Lay or sat or crouched.
And the miasma of their breathing
And of the odours of the night
Rose towards the radiant
And impassive heaven.

Night Piece

(Smyrna Harbour)

The stars stole out over the sea,
And the ghostly moon deepened to a silver crescent,
And the crimson ardours of sunset died lingeringly
In brooding haze of tender green and gold,
And the hills faded into dimness and dream.
And amid the velvet darkness
And soft scented airs
Of the Spring night
A myriad gleams twinkled:
The lights of the town answering the far-sprinkled heavens
From as mysterious blackness,
The shadowy shipping scintillating with points of fire,
That the dark water
Gave back quivering,

The lights on the terraced hills climbing to meet the stars,
Till the far-spreading night palpitated as with fallen stars
That had netted themselves in rigging
And dipped themselves in ocean
And found a home for their shining in the folds of the hills.
And in the great ship anchored in the quiet bay,
The sounds of chatter and scuffle,
Of Greek songs and Arab prayers,
Fell fainter and fainter,
Till the last wakeful occupant of the swarming steerage
Passed from the sense of his discomfort and his sorrows
Into the silence and peace
Of the many-twinkling night.

Prologue to "The Revolted Daughter"

To sea-sick souls on board our storm-tossed day
A fellow-passenger presents his play.
'Tis not that he aspires with midnight oil
To lull the seas that seethe, the waves that boil;
Enough if for a space he turn your minds
From thoughts of shipwreck and the shrieking winds.
For 'though 'twixt Heaven and Hell our bark be cast
The Comic Muse bestrides the giddy mast,
Watches the gale, a twinkle in her eye,
Assured, whate'er befall, not she will die,
Nor howso bound, to whatsoever port,
Shall mortals fail of antics for her sport.
Dost dream their sainthood would erase her grin,
Though Politicians brought Millennium in?
Till tired Time has dropped his blunted sickle
Their jests shall sadden and their wisdoms tickle.
Too long, too long she's eyed the human show
To look for perfect creatures here below.
Rome, Athens, Paris, London, she has watched,
And always known the human being botched.
However great and good and wise and clever,
Yet flesh and blood is flesh and blood for ever.
Diversely mad, men variously rave,
But sleep alike in cradle, bed, and grave.
And so the Comic Muse finds no attraction
In fad or ism, party-creed or faction;
She's lost her faith in all except Reaction.
She understands the failure of success,
And disbelieves in Progress by Express,
And Revolution—christened not in vain,
For the old thing comes always round again.
And yet she is not all malicious sneer,
Her tricksiest smile is tempered by a tear,

Making a Rainbow o'er our ruined earth,
And promising, as at the Rainbow's birth,
That all things shall continue—sun and rain,
Seed-time and harvest, death and love and pain.
So spite the croakers or the rhapsodists
Whose promised land is veiled in mellow mists,
'Tis Humour's rainbow spans our mortal life,
Arching the gloom, enlightening the strife,
A pledge, though darkness smite our wintry sphere,
That sun and moon are dead we need not fear,
Nor be, though earth's foundations shake, afraid
The songs of birds shall fail or flowers fade,
Or be forgot the way of man with maid.

Prologue to "Children of the Ghetto"

Behold, O friends, who stern in judgment sit,
A hidden world the footlights ne'er have lit:
A world whose day and night, whose sun and shade,
By spinning round the ancient Law are made;
Whose springs and winters take—whate'er the clime—
From old Jerusalem their changeless time.
Still in God's love the chosen people basks,
But ah! what tragic price Jehovah asks.
How strange a miracle this deathless life,
Aye with itself and all the world at strife—
This life that links us to the purple past
Of Babylon and Egypt, all the vast
Enchantment of the ancient Orient,
And yet with London and New York is blent;
The life that lives, though Greece and Rome are dust,
And Spain's inquisitorial racks are rust;
And though so faded from the ancient glory,
When Kings and Prophets shone in Israel's story,
Is brightening once again, yet who shall say
With light of Eastern or of Western day?
Our drama shows a phase transitional,
Young love at war with ancient ritual—
How dead laws living, loving hearts may fetter,
The contest of the Spirit and the Letter.
Yet noble, too, that kissing of the rod,
That stern obedience to the word of God,
In godless days when sweated Hebrews scout
The faith their sunless lives are dark without.
But do not deem the Ghetto is all gloom!
The Comic Spirit mocks the ages' doom,
And weaves athwart the woof of tragic drama
The humours of the human panorama.
The poet vaunts, the hypocrite goes supple,

The marriage-broker mates the bashful couple,
The peddler cries his wares, the player aces,
Saint jostles sinner, fun with wisdom paces,
The beggars prosper and the babes increase,
And over all the Sabbath whispers, "Peace!"

The Hebrew's Friday Night

(After Burns)

"Come, my beloved, to meet the Bride; the Face of the Sabbath let us welcome."

Sweet Sabbath-Bride, the Hebrew's theme of praise,
Celestial maiden with the starry eyes,
Around thine head a sacred nimbus plays,
Thy smile is soft as lucent summer skies,
Before thy purity all evil dies.
In wedding-robe of stainless sunshine drest,
Thou dawnest on Life's darkness and it dies;
Thy bridal-wreath is lilies Heaven-blest,
Thy dowry Peace and Love and Holiness and Rest.
For in thy Presence he forgets awhile
The gloom and discord of man's mortal years,
To seek the Light that streameth from thy Face,
To list thy tender lullaby, which cheers
His soul and lies like music on his ears.
His very sorrows with soft splendour shine,
Transfigured by a mist of sacred tears;
He drinks thy gently-offered Anodyne
And feels himself absorbed into the Peace divine.
The Father from the Synagogue returns
(A singing-bird is nestling at his heart),
And from without the festive light discerns
Which tells his faithful wife has done her part
To welcome Sabbath with domestic art.
He enters and perceives the picture true,
And tears unbidden from his eyelids start,
As Paradise thus opens on his view,
And then he smiles and thanks his God he is a Jew.
For "Friday-night" is written on his home
In fair, white characters; his wife has spread
The snowy Sabbath-cloth; the Hebrew tome,
The flask and cup are at the table's head,
There's Sabbath magic in the very bread,
And royal fare the humble dishes seem;
A holy light the Sabbath candles shed,
Around his children's shining faces beam,
He feels the strife of every day a far-off dream.
His buxom wife he kisses, then he lays

Upon each child's young head two loving hands
Of benediction, so in after days,
When they shall be afar in other lands,
They shall be knit to God and home by bands
Of sacred memory. And then he makes
The blessing o'er the wine, and while each stands,
The quaintly convoluted bread he breaks,
Which tastes to all to-night more sweet than honeyed cakes.
And now they eat the Sabbath meal with laugh
And jest and gossip till all fun must cease,
While Father chants the Grace, all singing half,
And then the Sabbath hymns of Love and Peace
And Hope from alien lands to find release.
No evil can this night its head uprear,
Earth's joys loom larger and its ills decrease;
To-night of ghosts the youngest has no fear—
Does not his guardian Sabbath Angel hover near?
So in a thousand squalid Ghettos penned,
Engirt yet undismayed by perils vast,
The Jew in hymns that marked his faith would spend
This night and dream of all his glorious Past
And wait the splendours by his seers forecast.
And so while mediæval creeds at strife
With nature die, the Jew's ideals last,
The simple love of home and child and wife,
The sweet humanities which make our higher life.

Seder-Night

Prosaic miles of streets stretch all around
Astir with restless, hurried life and spanned
By arches that with thund'rous trains resound,
And throbbing wires that galvanize the land;
Gin-palaces in tawdry splendour stand;
The news-boys shriek of mangled bodies found;
The last burlesque is playing in the Strand—
In modern prose all poetry seems drowned.
Yet in ten thousand homes this April night
An ancient People celebrates its birth
To Freedom, with a reverential mirth,
With customs quaint and many a hoary rite,
Waiting until, its tarnished glories bright,
Its God shall be the God of all the earth.

Israel As Bride and As Beggar

(From the Hebrew of Elchanan ben Isaac, an English Jew of the twelfth century, preserving the acrostic of the author's name)

Erst radiant the Bride adored,
On whom rich wedding gifts are poured,
She weeps, sore wounded, overthrown,
Exiled and outcast, shunned and lone.
Laid all aside her garments fair,
The pledges of a bond divine,
A wandering beggar-woman's wear
Is hers in lieu of raiment fine.
Chaunted hath been in every land
The beauty of her crown and zone;
Now doomed, dethroned, she maketh moan,
Bemocked—a byword—cursed and banned.
AN airy, joyous step was hers
Beneath Thy wing. But now she crawls
Along and mourns her sons and errs
At every step, and, worn out, falls.
And yet to Thee she clingeth tight,
Vain, vain to her man's mortal might
Which in a breath to naught is hurled,
Thy smile alone makes up her world.

The Jews of England (1290-1902)

An Edward's England spat us out—a band
Foredoomed to redden Vistula or Rhine,
And leaf-like toss with every wind malign.
All mocked the faith they could not understand.
Six centuries have passed. The yellow brand
On shoulder nor on soul has left a sign,
And on our brows must Edward's England twine
Her civic laurels with an equal hand.
Thick-clustered stars of fierce supremacy
Upon the martial breast of England glance!
She seems of War the very Deity.
Could aught remain her glory to enhance?
Yea, for I count her noblest victory
Her triumph o'er her own intolerance.

Melisselda (Turkish Messiah's Song)

There the Emperor's daughter
Lay agleam in the water,
Melisselda.
And its breast to her breast

Lay in tremulous rest,
Melisselda.
From her bath she arose
Pure and white as the snows,
Melisselda.
Coral only at lips
And at sweet finger-tips,
Melisselda.
In the pride of her race
As a sword shone her face,
Melisselda.
And her lids were steel bows,
But her mouth was a rose,
Melisselda.

Zionist Marching Song

(From the Hebrew of Imber)

I

"Like the crash of the thunder
Which splitteth asunder
The flame of the cloud,
On our ears ever falling,
A voice is heard calling
From Zion aloud:
'Let your spirits' desires
For the land of your sires
Eternally burn.
From the foe to deliver
Our own holy river,
To Jordan return.'
Where the soft-flowing stream
Murmurs low as in dream,
There set we our watch.
Our watchword 'The sword
Of our land and our Lord—'
By Jordan there set we our watch.

II

"Rest in peace, lovèd land,
For we rest not, but stand,
Off shaken our sloth.
When the bolts of war rattle
To shirk not the battle,
We make thee our oath.

As we hope for a Heaven,
Thy chains shall be riven,
Thine ensign unfurled.
And in pride of our race
We will fearlessly face
The might of the world.
When our trumpet is blown
And our standard is flown,
Then set we our watch.
Our watchword, 'The sword
Of our land and our Lord—'
By Jordan then set we our watch.

III

"Yea, as long as there be
Birds in air, fish in sea,
And blood in our veins;
And the lions in might,
Leaping down from the height,
Shake, roaring, their manes;
And the dew nightly laves
The forgotten old graves
Where Judah's sires sleep,
We swear, who are living,
To rest not in striving,
To pause not to weep.
Let the trumpet be blown,
Let the standard be flown,
Now set we our watch.
Our watchword, 'The sword
Of our land and our Lord'—
By Jordan now set we our watch."

Yom Kippur

I saw a people rise before the sun,
A noble people scattered through the lands,
To be a blessing to the nations, spread
Wherever mortals make their home; without
A common soil and air, 'neath alien skies,
But One in blood and thought and life and law,
And One in righteousness and love, a race
That, permeating, purified the world—
A pure fresh current in a brackish sea,
A cooling wind across the fevered sand,
A music in the wrangling market-place;
For wheresoe'er a Jew dwelt, there dwelt Truth,

And wheresoe'er a Jew was, there was Light,
And wheresoe'er a Jew went, there went Love.
This people saw I shake off sleep, ere flamed
The sunrise of Atonement Day, and haste,
The rich and poor alike, the old and young,
Each from his house unto the House of God,
The whole race closelier knit that day by one
Electric thought that flashed through all the world.
And there from dawn to sunset, and beyond,
They prayed, and wept, and fasted for their few
Backslidings from the perfect way; for they
Did Justice and loved Mercy, and with God
Walked humbly; Pride and Scorn they knew not; Lust
Of Gold or Power darkened not their souls;
The faces of the poor they did not grind,
But lived as Man with Man; yet all the day
In self-abasement did they pray and fast.
The ancient tongue of patriarchs and seers,
A golden link that bound them to the Past,
Was theirs; as woven by their saints
And rabbis into wondrous songs of praise
And sorrow; sad, remorseful strains, and sweet,
Soft, magic words of comfort. As they prayed,
They meditated on the words they spake,
And thought of those who wrote them—royal souls
In whom the love of Zion flamed; poets clad
Not in the purple, sages scorning not
The cobbler's bench; and then they mused on all
The petty yet not unheroic lives
Of those who, spite of daily scorn, in face
Of sensual baits, kept fast the marriage-vows
Which they in youth had pledged their Bride, the Law,
Whom they had taken to their hearths; no spirit
Austere and mystic, cold and far away,
But human-eyed, for mortal needs create,
Who linked her glory with their daily lives,
Bringing a dowry not unblent with tears—
A marriage made in Heaven to hallow Earth.
They thought of countless martyrs scorning life
Weighed 'gainst their creed; poor, simple workmen made
Imperial by their empery of pain;
Who clomb the throne of fire and draped themselves
In majesty of flame, and haughtily
As king for king awaited Death's approach.
The inspiration of such lives as these
Was on the worshippers; the stormy passion
Of their old, rugged prophets filled their hearts
With yearning, aspiration infinite,
Submerging puny fears about themselves,
Their individual fates in either world,
In one vast consciousness of Destiny.

For other Faiths, like glowworms glittering,
Had come to lift the darkness; and were dark.
And other Races, splendid in their might,
Had flashed upon the darkness and were gone.
But they had stood; a Tower all the waves
Of all the seas confederate could not shake;
And in the Tower a perpetual light
Burned, an eternal witness to the Hand
That lit it. So all day they prayed and wept
And fasted. And the sun went down, and night
Came on; and twilight filled the House of God,
And the gray dusk seemed filled with floating shapes
Of prophets and of martyrs lifting hands
Of benediction. Then a mighty voice
Arose and swelled, and all the bent forms swayed,
As when a wind roars, shaking all the trees
In some dim forest, and from every throat
Went up with iteration passionate
The watchword of the Host of Israel,
"The Lord our God is one! The Lord is God!
The Lord is God!" And suddenly there came
An awful silence. Then the trumpet's sound
Thrilled. . . .
And I awoke, for lo! it was a dream.

A Tabernacle Thought

Lovely grapes and apples,
And such pretty flowers,
Blooming in the Succah,
That in the back-yard towers.
Green leaves for the ceiling
Sift the sun and shade
To a pretty pattern,
As in forest glade.
Cool retreat and dainty
For a little child,
Toddling in, by prospect
Of its joys beguiled.
Round he casts his blue eyes,
Stretches hand in haste;
Darling baby, all this
Just is to his taste.
But his eyes brim over
Soon with sudden tears.
Ah, he learns the lesson
Of the coming years.
For the fruit is gilded
And the flowers are wax.

Life's a pretty vision,
Only truth it lacks.

Israel in Exile: or Harlequin Little Jacob Horner

("By a coincidence the orthodox Jew will begin the twentieth century with a fast in commemoration of the beginning of the Siege of Jerusalem."—Jewish Chronicle)

A whit long-spun, O Lord, the epic play,
"The Wandering Jew" in nineteen hundred acts,
Too dizzying with whirligig of facts;
We relish briefer tragedies to-day.
Yet less the bloody episodes dismay
With sense of doom and void prophetic pacts,
And less the Ghetto-gloom the heart contracts
Than this gay ending of the weary way.
This transformation scene where hero-saint
Gives place to prancing clown and pantaloon,
And Comus crews in masquerading paint,
No more for Zion crying—but the moon.
Messiah's heart itself will surely faint.
How rally these? With Shofar or bassoon?

Moses and Jesus

Methought on two Jews meeting I did chance—
One old, stern-eyed, deep-browed; yet garlanded
With living light of love around his head;
The other young, with sweet, seraphic glance.
Round them went on the Town's satanic dance,
Hunger a-piping while at heart he bled.
Shalom Aleikhem mournfully each said,
Nor eyed the other straight, but looked askance.
Sudden from Church outrolled an organ hymn,
From Synagogue a loudly-chaunted air,
Each with its Prophet's high acclaim instinct.
Then for the first time met their eyes swift-linked
In one strange, silent, piteous gaze, and dim
With bitter tears of agonized despair.

Israel

Hear, O Israel, Jehovah, the Lord our God is One,
But we, Jehovah His people, are dual and so undone.
Slaves in eternal Egypts, baking their strawless bricks,

At ease in successive Zions, prating their politics;
Rotting in sunlit Roumania, pigging in Russian Pale,
Driving in Park, Bois and Prater, clinging to Fashion's tail;
Reeling before every rowdy, sore with a hundred stings,
Clothed in fine linen and purple, loved at the courts of Kings;
Faithful friends to our foemen, slaves to a scornful clique,
The only Christians in Europe, turning the other cheek;
Priests of the household altar, blessing the bread and wine,
Lords of the hells of Gomorrah, licensed keepers of swine;
Coughing o'er clattering treadles, saintly and underpaid,
Ousting the rough from Whitechapel—by learning the hooligan's trade;
Pious, fanatical zealots, throttled by Talmud-coil,
Impious, lecherous sceptics, cynical stalkers of spoil;
Wedded 'neath Hebrew awning, buried 'neath Hebrew sod,
Between not a dream of duty, never a glimpse of God;
Risking our lives for our countries, loving our nations' flags,
Hounded therefrom in repayment, hugging our bloody rags;
Blarneying, shivering, crawling, taking all colours and none,
Lying a fox in the covert, leaping an ape in the sun.
Tantalus-Proteus of Peoples, security comes from within!
Where is the lion of Judah? Wearing an ass's skin!
Hear, O Israel, Jehovah, the Lord our God is One,
But we, Jehovah His people, are dual and so undone.

Jehovah

"Destroying and making alive, and causing salvation to spring forth."—Jewish Prayer-Book

I sing the uplift and the upwelling,
I sing the yearning towards the sun,
And the blind sea that lifts white hands of prayer.
I sing the wild battle-cry of warriors
And the sweet whispers of lovers,
The dear word of the hearth and the altar,
Aspiration, Inspiration, Compensation,God!
The hint of beauty behind the turbid cities,
The eternal laws that cleanse and cancel,
The pity through the savagery of nature,
The love atoning for the brothels,
The Master-Artist behind his tragedies,
Creator, Destroyer, Purifier, Avenger,God!
Come into the circle of Love and Justice,
Come into the brotherhood of Pity,
Of Holiness and Health!
Strike out glad limbs upon the sunny waters
Or be dragged down amid the rotting weeds,
The festering bodies.
Save thy soul from sandy barrenness,
Let it blossom with roses and gleam with the living waters.

Blame not, nor reason of your Past,
Nor explain to Him your congenital weakness,
But come, for He is remorseless,
Call Him unjust, but come.
Do not mock or defy Him, for He will prevail;
He regardeth not you; He hath swallowed the worlds and the nations;
He hath humour, too: disease and death for the smugly prosperous.
For such is the Law, stern, unchangeable, shining,
Making dung from souls and souls from dung,
Thrilling the dust to holy, beautiful spirit,
And returning the spirit to dust.
Come, and ye shall know Peace and Joy,
Let what ye desire of the Universe penetrate you,
Let Loving-kindness and Mercy pass through you,
And Truth be the Law of your mouth.
For so ye are channels of the divine sea,
Which may not flood the earth but only steal in
Through rifts in your souls.

Atonement Hymn

(By Yomtob of York. The translation of this curiosity of literature preserves, without adding or subtracting a single word, the precise metre, rhyme-scheme, and alphabetical acrostic of the twelfth-century Hebrew original. The Lily is one of the names for Israel)

*A*y 'tis thus	Evil us	hath in bond;
*B*y thy grace	guilt efface	and respond,
		"Forgiven!"
*C*ast scorn o'er	and abhor	th' Informer's word;
*D*ear God deign	this refrain	to make heard,
		"Forgiven!"
*E*ar in lieu	give him who	intercedes;
*F*avouring	answer, King,	when he pleads,
		"Forgiven!"
*G*rant also	the Lily blow	in Abram's right;
*H*eal our shame	and proclaim	from thine height,
		"Forgiven!"
*J*ust, forgiving,	Mercy living,	sin condone;
*L*ist our cry,	loud reply	from Thy Throne,
		"Forgiven!"
*M*y wound heal,	deep conceal	stain and flake,
*N*ow gain praise	by Thy phrase	For My sake,
		"Forgiven!"

O forgive!	Thy sons live	from thee reft;
Praised for grace.	Turn thy face	to those left—
		"Forgiven!"

Raise to Thee	this my plea,	take my pray'r,
Sin unmake	for Thy sake	and declare,
		"Forgiven!"

Tears, regret,	witness set	in Sin's place;
Uplift trust	from the dust	to Thy face—
		"Forgiven!"

Adon Olam

(Synagogue Hymn in the Original Metre)

Lord of the world, He reigned alone
While yet the Universe was naught.
When by His will all things were wrought,
Then first His sovran name was known.
And when the All shall cease to be,
In dread lone splendour He shall reign.
He was, He is, He shall remain
In glorious eternity.
For He is one, no second shares
His nature or His loneliness;
Unending and beginningless,
All strength is His, all sway He bears.
He is the living God to save,
My Rock while sorrow's toils endure,
My banner and my stronghold sure,
The cup of life whene'er I crave.
I place my soul within His palm,
Before I sleep as when I wake,
And though my body I forsake,
Rest in the Lord in fearless calm.

Israel Zangwill – A Short Biography

Israel Zangwill was born in London on 21st January 1864, to a family of Jewish immigrants from the Russian Empire. His father, Moses, was from modern-day Latvia, and his mother, Ellen Hannah Marks Zangwill, from modern-day Poland.

Zangwill was initially educated in Plymouth and Bristol. At age 9 he was enrolled into the Jews' Free School in Spitalfields in east London. The school was for the children of Jewish immigrants and added to its teaching, of both secular and religious matters, with supplies of clothing, food, and health care.

Zangwill excelled here. He began to teach part-time at the school and eventually full time. Whilst teaching he also studied with the University of London and by 1884 had earned his BA with triple honours in philosophy, history, and the sciences.

He had already co-written a tale entitled 'The Premier and the Painter' when he resigned as a teacher owing to differences with the managers of the school. Zangwill now turned to journalism for his new career path, initiating Ariel, The London Puck, as well as working in various capacities for the London press.

His writing earned him the sobriquet "the Dickens of the Ghetto" primarily based on his much lauded novel 'Children of the Ghetto: A Study of a Peculiar People' in 1892 and its glimpse of the poverty-stricken life in London's Jewish quarter.

As a writer he was keen to reflect on his political and social outlooks. His simulation of Yiddish sentence structure in English aroused great interest. His mystery work, 'The Big Bow Mystery' (1892) was the first locked room mystery novel. Social satire flowed with 'The King of Schnorrers' (1894). A follow up to 'Children of the Ghetto' was 'Ghetto Tragedies' in 1894 and 'Dreamers of the Ghetto' in 1898 which included essays on famous Jews such as Baruch Spinoza, Heinrich Heine and Ferdinand Lassalle.

Zangwill was also involved with narrowly focused Jewish issues as an assimilationist, an early Zionist, and later a territorialist. In the early 1890s he had joined the Lovers of Zion movement in England. A few years later, in 1897, he took part in the "pilgrimage" of English Jews to Palestine. That same year he also joined Theodor Herzl (considered the father of modern political Zionism) in founding the World Zionist Organization and would take part in the first seven Zionist congresses. Zangwill was much admired as an orator and spoke movingly and eloquently on the issues he was passionate on.

In 1901 he had written that "Palestine is a country without a people; the Jews are a people without a country". On Herzl's visits to London, they worked closely together. In a debate at the Article Club in November 1901 however Zangwill was still mis-using the facts: "Palestine has but a small population of Arabs and fellahin and wandering, lawless, blackmailing Bedouin tribes." And made a direct plea to "restore the country without a people to the people without a country. For we have something to give as well as to get. We can sweep away the blackmailer—be he Pasha or Bedouin—we can make the wilderness blossom as the rose, and build up in the heart of the world a civilisation that may be a mediator and interpreter between the East and the West."

In 1902, Zangwill wrote that Palestine "remains at this moment an almost uninhabited, forsaken and ruined Turkish territory". But from this point on Zangwill began to see things differently which would, in 1905, result in his breakaway from Zionism.

Zangwill quit the established philosophy of Zionism when his plan for a homeland in Uganda was rejected and instead founded his own organisation; the Jewish Territorialist Organization. Its stated goal was to create a Jewish homeland in whatever territory in the world could be found for them. At that point in time suggestions were as varied as Canada, Australia, Mesopotamia, Argentina, Uganda and Cyrenaica.

Amongst the challenges in his life he found time to write poetry. He had translated a medieval Jewish poet in 1903 and his own volume 'Blind Children' in 1908 shows his promise in this new endeavour.

In 1908, Zangwill told a London court that he had been naive when he made his 1901 speech and had since recognised that the Arab population was twice that of the United States.

Zangwill was a supporter of both feminism and pacifism, but his greatest effect was as a writer who gained a wide audience with the idea of combining ethnicities into a single, American nation. The hero of 'The Melting Pot', proclaims: "America is God's Crucible, the great Melting-Pot where all the races of Europe are melting and reforming... Germans and Frenchmen, Irishmen and Englishmen, Jews and Russians – into the Crucible with you all! God is making the American."'

'The Melting Pot' made Zangwill's name as an admired playwright. The title itself was popularised as the phrase to use to describe American absorption of immigrants when it ran in the United States.

When the play opened in Washington D.C. on 5th October 1909, former President Theodore Roosevelt leaned over the edge of his box and shouted, "That's a great play, Mr. Zangwill, that's a great play." In a later letter in 1912 Roosevelt went further "That particular play I shall always count among the very strong and real influences upon my thought and my life."

'The Melting Pot' shone a spotlight on America's growth through the input of its new waves of immigrants. Zangwill was writing as "a Jew who no longer wanted to be a Jew. His real hope was for a world in which the entire lexicon of racial and religious difference is thrown away."

According to Ze'ev Jabotinsky, Zangwill told him in 1916 that, "If you wish to give a country to a people without a country, it is utter foolishness to allow it to be the country of two peoples. This can only cause trouble. The Jews will suffer and so will their neighbours. One of the two: a different place must be found either for the Jews or for their neighbours".

In 1917 he wrote "'Give the country without a people,' magnanimously pleaded Lord Shaftesbury, 'to the people without a country.' Alas, it was a misleading mistake. The country holds 600,000 Arabs."

With the end of World War I, and a more clearly defined idea of a Jewish settlement in Palestine, Zangwill once more returned to the Zionist effort and made efforts on behalf of the Balfour Declaration, proclaiming the right of a Jewish homeland in Palestine

In 1921 Zangwill wrote "If Lord Shaftesbury was literally inexact in describing Palestine as a country without a people, he was essentially correct, for there is no Arab people living in intimate fusion with the country, utilizing its resources and stamping it with a characteristic impress: there is at best an Arab encampment, the break-up of which would throw upon the Jews the actual manual labor of regeneration and prevent them from exploiting the fellahin, whose numbers and lower wages are moreover a considerable obstacle to the proposed immigration from Poland and other suffering centers".

Despite his advocacy on Jewish matters he would be disappointed to know that despite Israel now being established the quarrels of the Middle East continue to divide.

Israel Zangwill died on 1st August 1926 in Midhurst, West Sussex.

Israel Zangwill – A Concise Bibliography

The Bachelors' Club (1891)

The Old Maid's Club (1892)
Children of the Ghetto: A Study of a Peculiar People (1892)
Grandchildren of the Ghetto (1892)
The Big Bow Mystery (1892)
Merely Mary Ann (1893)
The King of Schnorrers (1894)
The Master (1895) (based on the life of George Wylie Hutchinson)
Without Prejudices (1896)
Dreamers of the Ghetto (1898)
Ghetto Tragedies, (1899)
"The Return to Palestine", New Liberal Review, (Dec. 1901)
Children of the Ghetto (1902)
"Providence, Palestine and the Rothschilds", The Speaker, vol. 4, no. 125 (22 February 1902)
Selected Religious Poems (1903) Translation of the Jewish Medieval Poet Solomon in Cabirol.
The Grey Wig: Stories and Novelettes (1903)
The Serio-Comic Governess (1904)
Merely Mary Ann (1904)
Ghetto Comedies, (1907)
Blind Children (1908) Poetry
The Melting Pot (1909)
Italian Fantasies (1910) Travel
Chosen Peoples, (1919)
The War For The World (1916)
The Principle of Nationalities (1917)
Chosen Peoples (1918)
Hands Off Russia: Speech by Mr. Israel Zangwill at the Albert Hall, February 8th, 1919. London: Workers' Socialist Federation, n.d. (1919)
The Voice of Jerusalem. (1921)

Filmography

Children of the Ghetto (1915, based on the play Children of the Ghetto)
The Melting Pot (1915, based on the play The Melting Pot)
Merely Mary Ann (1916, based on the play Merely Mary Ann)
The Moment Before (1916, based on the play The Moment of Death)
Mary Ann (1918, based on the play Merely Mary Ann)
Nurse Marjorie (1920, based on the play Nurse Marjorie)
Merely Mary Ann (1920, based on the play Merely Mary Ann)
The Bachelor's Club (1921, based on the novel We Moderns)
We Moderns (1925, based on the play We Moderns)
Too Much Money (1926, based on the play Too Much Money)
Perfect Crime (1928, based on the novel The Big Bow Mystery)
Merely Mary Ann (1931, based on the play Merely Mary Ann)
The Crime Doctor (1934, based on the novel The Big Bow Mystery)
The Verdict (1946, based on the novel The Big Bow Mystery)